Honeysuckle and Roses

Other Books
by Jody Anne Iodice

A Forensic Clinical Training Manual: Introduction to the Forensic Field, The Study of Psychological Trauma and Victimology

Honeysuckle and Roses

Jody Anne Iodice

BOOKLOGIX®
Alpharetta, GA

ISBN: 978-1-6653-0676-8 - Paperback
eISBN: 978-1-6653-0677-5 - eBook

Library of Congress Control Number: 2024914713

⊚This paper meets the requirements of ANSI/NISO Z39.48-1992 (Permanence of Paper)

1 1 1 1 2 5

To my parents, who throughout their lives, taught me by their examples that creative expression of any kind is the key to living a life of contentment, happiness, and joy.

t all happened on one of our typical steamy, hot, Mississippi-Delta, August afternoons, where the stale, smoldering humidity hangs in the air and stifles any breeze that may come our way. Bless my heart, I believe my mama knew I had just too much sadness, too much pain, and too much resentment that day. I should point out that some said it happened because of the un-relenting, muggy heat of our late Mississippi summer. It gets really hot in Cypress Groves, Mississippi, especially in August. On that sweltering, hot, and sticky August day at around 1:30 p.m., with the intense drum-like sounds of those Coastal Scissor Grinder Cicadas summer song ever present in the background, someone or something stepped in and took a hold of me—but I believe I know who it was. And on that day, the balance of power shifted.

As I was trying to shake my shoes free from the puddle of sticky, chocolate-colored blood that had soaked the rubber sole of my white, Keds sneakers, I walked slowly over to the kitchen phone, the one that hung on the wall by the doorway between the kitchen and the living room. It was a bright butter-yellow color with a long, twisted, plastic cord of the same color that reached as far as the living room table. That's where I sat to call him.

"Sheriff Louie, this is Benevolence Mae, and I need to inform you that Mr. Beals is dead on *my* living room floor," I offered, matter-of-factly.

ᔕᐧᔕᐧᔕᐧ

Before I go any further about the story, I know you're saying, "Wait a minute, you can't leave me hanging like that, what happened?!" Well, I'll get to that, but we—yes, *we*— Sheriff Louis Frances Roulette and myself, Benevolence Mae Pumpkin—believe it would be better if you knew a bit about my life here in Cypress Groves, Mississippi, and my people before I tell you what happened.

So, you see, I'm the only daughter and only child of Beauty Eveline Pumpkin and Natchez Jerimiah Pumpkin and . . . we are Black. My parents were both born and bred right here, in Cypress Groves, Mississippi. My mama and daddy, they are both now long since gone, yet only an arm's reach across the "veil" that separates us four. Yes, me and Sheriff Louie are on the earthly side of that veil. Sheriff Louie and I, that's what we call him down here in Cypress Groves, will be telling y'all about how our lives became interwoven with my mama's. But the crux of the story we are about to tell y'all . . . well sho'nuff, some of y'all are going to be pretty skeptical of. I'm as sure of that as I am about the right spices to boil Mississippi Blue Crabs with. However, for Sheriff Louie and me, what took

2

place on that August afternoon in the suffocating heat so typical to Cypress Groves, Mississippi, did not shake us. See, I grew up with what's called down here in the Mississippi marsh as a *"Spirit knowing ways."* Ya see, I have been imbued with this power of the Spirit to know realms beyond this earth . . . where those realms are porous and no separation of time or space exists between them, and the answers to questions and thoughts of others are transparent to me at any moment in time. And Sheriff Louie — well, I'll let him tell you a bit later on about his own understanding of the veil between the dimensions of past, and present, and future, transcending all time and space.

But now, I'd like to tell y'all a little more about myself; my mama, Beauty Pumpkin, and my daddy, Natchez Pumpkin, and that ole White man, Mr. Ezekiel Beals. As I told you, my name is Benevolence Mae. When I was just a little thing, I would go with Mama to the market in town, and I could hear folks whisper to each other as Mama and I passed them by . . . *"She's not right in the head, that little one."* I saw how folks looked at me kind of apprehensive and they dashed to the side, away from me, so as not to get too close. Simultaneously, I would feel my mama's hand just squeeze around my little fingers and she would smile down at me approvingly, and then bend down and whisper in my ear, *"Don't pay no mind to them, Benevolence Mae."* I think I worried folks, because even as a small child I moved slow-like, but not because I was lazy. I was trying to make sense of all the information that was coming to me from "out there." So, often, I did not speak a word, and my gaze upon folks would be focused on them — and that, understandably, unnerved them, but it was just that I was deeply pondering all the vibrating energy that I saw

3

swirling and darting around them. *"Not right for a child to be creeping around a person like that . . . and so silent, always peering at ya,"* they would say just loud enough for my mama and me to hear.

How people experienced me made them believe I was a "peculiar child" and others who knew I had "the Spirit special knowing ways," said they were just plain scared of my special sight. Those folks would see me coming their way, and they would lickety-split and cross the street as quickly as if they saw a skunk waddling toward them with his tail stiff and straight up in the air, ready to spray them with their stinky fumes. It made me laugh 'cause I thought to myself, *Good Lord, they should be more scared of an ole skunk than of me.*

Clearly, l was like no other Black child in Cyprus Groves, Mississippi. The elder Black folks who cared about me and lived along the banks of the Mississippi marsh called what I had, "distant knowing ways". They would say of me: *"That chil' can't help herself, she just born into this world invested with spiritual powers beyond these earthly realms . . . she knows 'bout everything and 'bout everybody that crosses her path before they speak to her. She's got it just like her daddy, Natchez, does! Those knowing ways born into her from her daddy."*

Yet, ever since I was just a little thing, wearing my sleeveless, pink, cotton sundresses Mama bought me at Belk's Department Store, and my sparkling, white lace ankle socks with pink, little roses on the edges tucked into my shiny, leather, lace-up Buster Browns, those who knew better—why, they just saw me as a child who had special gifts beyond what any of them could ever imagine having at my age. Thankfully, those folks would tell me right out I was most *"beautifully unusual with special sight and knowing."*

It was because of folks like that, and especially my mama, that I didn't think I was too odd. Even as a young'un, I could tell you what you were thinking before you dared speak it! My mama would say I could look a grown man in the eye and, "*With a penetrating gaze from those clear, watery-blue eyes of yours as dazzling and luminous as any topaz gemstone, Benevolence, chil', you'll stall him in his tracks, putting a cold sweat of apprehension upon him.*" My mama would chuckle when she said that to me. But most of all, I remember such a beautiful smile would cross her face and she would cup her hand upon my chin so gently and lovingly and bend down real low, looking into my eyes, and so softly and sweetly say to me, "My Benevolence Mae, you are my special little one, and you possess God's special gifts of knowing. He's going to look out for you, and since He just lent you to me while we's both here on earth, why, I'm going to do just that . . . no matter where I am . . . nobody's going to cross you . . . and don't you ever forget that, my darling."

When l spoke, you'd wonder where I came from because I sho'nuff didn't speak like any other of the Black children from the Mississippi marsh—nor the White children of the Mississippi marsh for that matter either. It was because my mama, Miss Beauty Eveline Pumpkin, had me carefully and correctly pronouncing words straight from Webster's Dictionary and reading the definitions by the time I was four. By age six, I was reciting with perfect diction and intonation the poetry of Mr. Sidney Lanier. Mama would say to me, "*Benevolence Mae, baby girl, I want you to have book-knowing ways too so you can take care of yourself by making your own way in this old world and do it without no man hovering over ya, telling ya what to do.*"

When I was around eight years old, I was aware I had

been pondering three things for some time. And so, one day, I asked my mama these three questions: *"Mama, will you tell me about my daddy? How did my daddy die? And how is it we came to live here with Mr. Ezekiel Beals . . . a White man?"* See, my daddy died when I was just three years old, and I had little memory of him. So, my mama answered those three questions of mine.

She told me about my daddy: *"Chil', your daddy, oh my, he had the most beautiful, bright, glistening, twinkling green eyes and a big, sweet, handsome smile too . . . just like yours; he towered over most men at six feet, five inches, with strong broad shoulders; and though most folks where a bit weary of your daddy 'cause how he was built so strong and 'cause of his 'special knowing ways,' he was a gentle man with kind ways, especially to both you and me, Benevolence Mae. And my sweet little Miss Benevolence Mae, you inherited those 'special gifts' from your daddy."*

Now here's the interesting part, many times when I was a child and my mama was still alive, she would gently touch my forehead with her fingertips, and she would say to me, *"The knowing ways will be something you'll have, right here, from your daddy, always."* So, it seems my daddy had those special knowing ways too and that's where I got them—from him. And so, it was that my daddy, Natchez Jeremiah Pumpkin, worked for Mr. Ezekiel Beals, a White man of course, clearing fields, planting crops, and whatever else Mr. Beals needed on his two-hundred-acre farmland.

It happened on one of our blazing hot Mississippi July summer days when, apparently, my daddy was clearing a field. Mama said she often would say to Daddy with much exasperation, *"Now, Natchez, that ole John Deere tracker of Mr. Beals is always breaking down. Can't ya tell him it's time for a new one? I worrys about yous on that thing."* And many times, indeed, my daddy had told ole Ezekiel Beals he might want to consider buying himself a new John Deere. But, of course, Mr. Beals would hear none of that—especially not from a "hired hand" and sho'nuff not from my daddy, *"a Blacky"* as Mr. Beals would call him right to his face! So, unfortunately, tragedy struck that hot sorrowful day in July. The gears on that ole John Deere tractor slipped, causing Daddy to lose control of the steering and the tractor veered off and pitched a hard right going down a long, deep slope in the pasture, gaining uncontrollable speed. It toppled and turned over into a deep, muddy-water gully at the bottom of the pasture. The tractor landed on my daddy, crushed him to death, and drowned him in those muddy waters.

And here's the most fascinating part of the day my daddy died. Mama told me, *"Those knowing ways are powerful, little girl, so powerful your sweet daddy knew when his time was coming and exactly when he was going to meet his maker! Your daddy woke beside me with a startle in the morning on that dreadful day and looked at me with those soulful, soft green-twinkling eyes of his and said to me just as calm-like as I'm talking to yous, 'My darling, Beauty, now, later today, is my day to meet our Maker! Beauty, I'll be dead by midday.'"*

Mama said Daddy seemed more scared for her than for himself and he was resigned and *"at peace"* with what was to come for him. *"Now, Beauty, what my knowing tells me is I won't suffer much, and it will be quick. I'm here to tell ya I am at peace about this, my darling. But here's what ya have to do, and I know there will be days it won't be easy, but yous and Benevolence are to stay on here with Mr. Ezekiel. Now, that White man sho'nuff won't take as good care of ya as I would, but I knows he will see to it that yous and our baby girl have a roof*

7

over y'alls heads and plenty of food in y'alls bellies. Of course, you be working for him just like yous always do around the house and in the vegetable garden and, of course, tending to yourn most beautiful rose garden. It will be better than if yous two are alone in this Mississippi marsh land, and it's this that my knowing tells me, my Beauty. We knows we must always follow the knowing ways. So, now, ya do as I say and nothing else!" Well, my mama told me she was shocked, scared, and a sadness took hold of her down to her soul that all rolled up in one big feeling of misery, but she knew my daddy was always right about these things and she had to accept what he told her. She said they both cried together for a few moments and my daddy held her tight for one last time, kissed her on her forehead, and before he walked out of life for good, Mama repeated to me Daddy's last words to her, *"'Beauty, I have always loved ya with every breath of my life and the last breath of my life and my last thoughts on this earth will be of yous and my little Benevolence Mae.' So, I did just as yourn daddy said I was to do as much as I wished it wasn't gonna be so."* And with that, my mama had answered all three of my questions and our life was forever changed on the day we came to live with Mr. Ezekiel Beals—without my daddy.

After my daddy's, Natchez, death, my mama and I came to live under the roof of Mr. Ezekiel Beals—and all that came with a racist White man of the Mississippi marsh who found favor in my mama's natural, stunning looks and shapely curves. My mama, although with a broken heart, endured it all for the sake of my welfare and even her own survival. Just like Daddy had told her to do because he *knew* it would have been worse for her as a beautiful young Black woman raising a small child, by herself, in the Mississippi Delta in the early 1960s. It would have been filled with dodging the hands of unholy Black and White men alike, doing whatever was called for to raise her child and keep food on the table—but was tending to one White man in his home and doing what was called for from his biding better? She chose the latter as my daddy had instructed her to do.

ಞಞಞ

As Benevolence said, the story we are about to share with you, well, you might say it sounds fanciful and un-likely, and you very well may be skeptical, but we are here to tell you it is a story of facts, a story of transcendence, redemption, and a story of alchemy. Yet, I too want you to know more about myself as well.

My name is Louis Frances Roulette, however, ever since I was a little boy my mother and grand-mère, Catalina, have called me Louie as does everyone else. I have been the sheriff in Cypress Groves, Mississippi, for nineteen years. And before that, I was the lone deputy for five years of Cypress Groves. This is the region of Mississippi known as the Lower Delta. Its marsh regions feed into the Mississippi River. Like most places in the rural south, there's the Black side of town and the White side of town. In Jackson County, the economic strata of residents is varied. Its people are either poor White folks or poor Black folks—that is—maybe they get lucky and have one meal in their bellies 'cause they had a good day of fishing in the marsh with a big catch of catfish, smallmouth bass, and redfish for frying up the family dinner. And then there are those White and Black folks just a bit above the poverty level— "marsh boat folks." They own their boats for fishing and rifles to hunt gators, but these "marsh boat" folks mainly hunt and kill alligators from the marshes of the region to sell their meat to the local markets. Folks down here in the Delta like their alligator stew! Then, there are the land-rich, cash-poor White folk, and then lastly, even fewer, White folk who are land-rich and money-rich. And these are the likes of Mr. Ezekiel Beals—more about Ezekiel a little later.

In Jackson County, many sheriffs before me were easily swayed by the constant manipulative attempts from wealthy White men of this county, who bribed them to overlook the likes of speeding tickets or vandalizing the stores in town by their drunken teenage sons or daughters. Therefore, although in their eyes I was the *right* race and gender, there were a lot of rich White men who didn't take to me when I first came to Cypress Groves as a young new lawman from New Or-leens, although just a deputy then. It was bad enough I couldn't be exploited by those wealthy White men with their wad of one hundred green-backs, but you see the second strike against me was I hailed from "the big, raucous, and sin-filled city of New Or-leens"—therefore I was considered *"an outsider,"* and the third strike against me from these so-called fine, up-standing, Christian Baptist, White, rich men of Cypress Groves, Mississippi, was that I came from a century-old French Cajun *Catholic* New Or-leens family. And there was the final and third strike against me. So, I wasn't sure what perturbed them more though—that they couldn't bribe me with their big money for "this or that" or that they thought when I was at Mass on Sundays *"with them Blackies"*—as there is only one Catholic Church in Cypress Groves—that those White rich men of Cypress Groves believed I was casting *"some hocus pocus French Cajun spell"* on them, while being blessed by the priest! I believe that bothered these men for years. Good Lord, I must admit I enjoyed keeping those fine, White, racist, "Christian" men guessing about me. Always made me laugh to myself.

Yes, y'all I'm a New Or-leens, French, Catholic Cajun going back five generations and since the age of three, I was steeped in bedtime tales from my grand-mère Catalina, about New Or-leens, French Cajun, Catholic Spiritualism; the chilling tales of the terrifying Rougarou, watching her concocting potions for the love-lorn or potions to recoup money from bad financial deals or gambling debts that wives wouldn't find out about, see her reading the herb leaves and shavings of sassafras roots from the bottom of tea-cups against cheating husbands, and hear the French Cajun chants for the healing of the sick. And it was to the home of my grand-mère Catalina that folks—men and women alike—came from parishes near and far to seek her out for her successful French Cajun incantations, prayers, and rituals. When the French doors leading to my grand-mère's library were closed, I knew I was not to go in as she was with someone helping and healing them with her *special Cajun ways*. But, all too often, I was curious as any little boy would be, and I would sneak ever so quickly down our long winding staircase from my bedroom, and I would stand motionless in front of those large, solid, mahogany French doors. I would hold my breath, trying to be ever so quiet, with my ear pressed to the French doors. And then, to my great surprise, I would hear that familiar French accent of hers— the sweet, loving, gentle, yet ever so firm voice of my grand-mère, *"Louie, mon ange scoot off now. Grand-mère Catalina is working."*

Quite astonished, I would think to myself, *How did she*

know I was here?! She always knows! How does she know so many things without seeing! How could she read people even before they speak to her!

It would only be later in my life that I would come to know more about my grand-mère Catalina's special, French Cajun, mystical ways. How my grand-mère Catalina saw, knew, and felt things beyond what any other person could see, know, or feel. And, to my surprise, when I was just five years old, my grand-mère Catalina called me to her library and sat me on her lap and told me: *"Louie Francis, as the Saints above have blessed me with a third sense of the mystical knowing and seeing, I see it in your soul and your eyes too, mon Louie. Mon chéri Louie, you too will know things about people before they even know it themselves and, petit Louie, you too will be able to foretell things before they happen . . . and you too will see things beyond even your own imaging . . . now listen to Grand-mère Catalina closely, chéri Louie, you are not to be fearful of this grand thing, as the Guard of Heavenly Saints and Angels above us are with you in these knowing ways always!"* and then she firmly emphasized my full name, cupped her beautiful hands around my cheeks, and said, *"Louie Frances, these special gifts that you too have — they are a gift from God, and we do not turn away gifts from God. You understand Grand-mère Catalina?"* And, of course, whatever my grand-mère Catalina told me, I did, and also, I knew it to be nothing but the holist of truth. You didn't question my grand-mère!

And so it was decreed to me that I too carried this *knowing—this "gift from God,"* as Grand-mère Catalina had told me about so many years ago—the ability to know things before they happened, to see things other people don't see, to hear what people were going to say before they say it, to read people's energy. It was all just as my grand-mère Catalina had told me . . . these *knowing visions and people's thoughts and words* blazoning in my head before they happened, before they were spoken . . . I *knew*.

It made me feel a little odd too as I was growing up. Somehow, I always felt just outside of everything yet was amongst everything. Just like when I was ten and, looking out my bedroom window, I saw my best friend, Charles Louis Gerard, hop on his bike. I always called him by his full name—and he called me Louis Frances . . . it's what we did. Charles Louis Gerard always rode his bike at breakneck speeds. In a second, I *saw* and I *knew* what was going to happen to Charles. A gray cat would dart out in front of him as he sped down the street and he would topple over on his bike and land hard on his right arm and leg, breaking both in multiple places . . . I wanted to yell at him so badly before he took off on his bike, but it all flashed before my eyes instantly, before I could even take a breath—and Grand-mère had also warned me, "*There will be times you must not interfere with God's work and cher petit-fils Louie you will also know when you can interfere.*" So, as I always followed her directions in such things, something told me not to interfere that morning. Charles Louis Gerard would spend the next two months sequestered to the bed in his room. I would come to visit and, together, we would read our favorite books, like *The Mouse and the Motorcycle* or *The Wolves of Willoughby Chase*, but mostly Charles Louis Gerard liked playing with his chemistry set. He became enthralled in executing chemistry experiments as a result. Charles Louis Gerard would later go on to Tulane University, major in microbiology, and then would continue on to Tulane Medical School, only to become re-nowned throughout the Southeast as a molecular infectious disease specialist. At lectures, he would credit his accomplishments and fascination with science to a gray cat, his "speed demon nature," and a fall from a bike he had at age ten!

As I got older, with my *"knowing ways"*, I came to be quite effective in navigating "being in the world but not of it", as my grand-mère Catalina had told me when I was a boy. She would add, "Mon chèri it will be this experience for you of swaddling two realms of being for the rest of your life" ... and it *was* just that for me ... and she was right! And I also got much better at understanding when to use my knowing ways, when to intervene in others lives, and when not to interfere—just as my grand-mère instructed me.

ഔഔഔ

So, how did I come to the remote rural, lower Delta of the Mississippi marsh from the Crescent City, where there had been plenty of job offers for me? I was just twenty-seven years old, and I was looking for solace, a new beginning. My beautiful young wife, of only twenty-four years old, was stricken with the ravages of what seemed like a never-ending, grueling, drawn-out illness. All the special gifts of Grand-mère Catalina could not save my precious Claudette Clare . . .

"But we will keep the maudit beast at bay for as long as we possibly can, mon amour Louie," Grand-mère Catalina would say to me. Grand-mère Catalina would give my Claudette potions and concoctions to keep her weight on, her skin glowing, her cheeks rosy, and her hair from thinning too much.

Yet, despite all that worked on the outside, 'the beast' was ravishing my sweet Claudette Clare on the inside, and

14

she was gone in just two years. *"The beast – Rougarou came a calling,"* my grand-mère would say. Claudette Clare would eventually lose all her wavy, lustrous chestnut-brown hair, her once sparkling, twinkling blue eyes became listless, vacant, and sunken, her peaches-and-cream radiant complexion grew sallow and grayish from the rounds of chemotherapy. These were memories I was desperate to forget and wanted to escape from.

I took the first job offer outside of New Or-leens that came my way and, with my freshly minted BS degree in Criminology from Louisiana State College, this was great news, but my heartache was so deep I had no idea those memories would follow me all across Lake Pontchartrain to the Mississippi Delta. Despite the heartache, I was driven and excited about working in a county populated with a White majority, and an underserved Black community, who had endured decades of injustice and violent acts of racism, while at the same time knowing I'd also be serving a fringe community of poor White folks who lived all along the Delta coast. They would be suspicious and mistrustful of "the lawman enforcing laws" against their *any* means of survival. This would be a fist full of varied challenges I was eager to face. So, there I was, this newly appointed deputy having just arrived in Jackson County, Mississippi, for the Cypress Groves Police Department, and five years later I was voted in as the new sheriff of Cypress Groves . . . and that happened because there was no one to run against me!

I would come to find the only person I could *not* hide my internal caldron of simmering loss from. Miss Beauty Eveline Pumpkin—this was Benevolence Mae's mama. Miss Beauty was the kindest, most decent, and generous woman I would come to know in Cypress Groves. She was a strikingly tall, dark-skinned Black woman, who was about ten years older than me. Didn't matter to her that I was a young White man from the "big city of New Orleens," nor did it matter to her that I was a "French Cajun Catholic," even though she was a Black woman living as far South as one could get in rural Mississippi's deep Delta. Her kind warm nature reminded me of my grand-mère Catalina. Over time, it would be Miss Beauty Pumpkin who would school me in the ways of Jackson county, *"Justice don't always find it's way here in Jackson County, Deputy Louie, especially between the White and Black folks. You best learn that now, son, and you'll do just fine in time."*

Miss Beauty Pumpkin, just like my grand-mère Catalina, knew that behind my six-foot, three-inch stature, congenial nature, and broad smile, was a man with a deep emptiness in his heart. Miss Beauty saw that emptiness that cast over me like the shade from one of our Mississippi towering water oak, with its vast, stretching branches casting shade on a sunny noonday. Miss Beauty Pumpkin always offered me an unexpected, unwavering kindness, as she knew I was new to the area, and Miss Beauty *knew* I needed an anchor of unspoken but welcomed kindness in an often unwelcoming place.

The very first time I would meet Miss Beauty Pumpkin, she endeared herself to me, and she didn't hold back anything neither. I was buying a Moon Pie in Earl Lee Abbot's market, and as I reached in my pocket for a dollar, a handful of quarters fell. I bent down to retrieve them but Miss Beauty was quicker than I and had already bent down and was scooping up those coins. Ever so gingerly, she handed them back to me, placing them in the palm of my outstretched hand, and cupping her hand gently over my palm and the coins. She said softly with a rich, kind, level tone in her voice and a twinkle in her blue-gray eyes, "*Now, son, my goodness that Moon Pie ain't enough to feed a stray dog. You come by the big house that sits back from County Road 428 when you can, and eats with me, my little girl, Benevolence, and Mr. Beals. Supper is always at six sharp. Yous don't even have to calls ahead . . . you just come on . . . ya here me, boy?*" As we both stood up, and I offered my hand to help her rise, Miss Beauty looked at me with her typical penetrating gaze, and I *knew* she was slowly studying my face and, most importantly, she was *reading my energy,* just like my grand-mère Catalina would do. I *knew* this would be a woman I was supposed to meet and a woman I could always trust.

The last thing Miss Beauty said to me when I was leaving Earl Lee's store will always stay with me. "*Now, you're young, Deputy Louie,*" —she called me Deputy Louie right from the start—"*and young hearts will mend, they sho'nuff do, but they heals better with a purpose to works at. I'm telling ya, son. You gots yourself a big purpose here in Cypress Groves. Yes, a big purpose you gots here in these parts, son. This marshland needs protecting from Black and White folks alike—foolish and evil don't know no color and the marsh gots some secrets that get people riled up. Your purpose here is taking care of all of us and that's gona help ya some, but not completely. So, when it don't, Deputy Louie, why—you just best get on your knees and tell the Good Lord you're putting your woes on his doorstep cause you can't handle the heartaches your carrying. You gotta let your purpose help you do your living and not live in the past. See, my life gots me my big purpose in raising my daughter, Benevolence Mae. My Benevolence Mae is a special little girl and that helps me some.*" Then Miss Beauty patted my arm and smiled at me with a kindness that lingered in her eyes, and then turned to walk out of Earl Lee's Market. Over her shoulder she called to me as she walked out the door, "*You have yourself a good day now, Deputy Louie, and know those troubles of yours, they gonna pass—its gonna takes some time, but its gonna get better. The Lord above see to it! You come by now and eats with us, soon as you can.*"

Yes, Miss Beauty Eveline Pumpkin with her typical laser-sharp understanding had found my heartache in our brief encounter, and from that day forward, when I saw her in town, happiness and peace and lightness would rise up in my chest. We would exchange a friendly, warm greeting like we were old friends who knew each other for years.

"*Hey, how ya doing, Deputy Louie?*" she'd ask me cheerfully.

"*I'm good today, Miss Beauty,*" I'd say and reply, "*And how are you doing today? Is there anything I can do for you, Miss Beauty?*"

Beauty would give me her characteristic, warm smile and reply joyfully, "*No, Deputy Louie, I don't need nothing but the prayers I got stashed in my pocket and the Lord above. But, if I needs ya for something down here, I'll call on ya sho'nuff!*" And she would be on her way with her characteristic, gentle smile, her ease, and grace. I always felt uplifted by those brief but formidable exchanges between us for the rest of my day. Miss Beauty Eveline Pumpkin made me feel like I belonged somewhere, even without Clare, and of all places it was in Cypress Grove, Mississippi.

That was it from that first day. We two seemed to be connected in our brokenness—it was palpable between us.

෨෨෨

In the years that followed her mother's death, what I came to know directly from Benevolence was that she found silence or just speaking a few words to exchange a thought most comforting. However, in living with Ezekiel, her silent nature would particularly disturb and unnerve him. Benevolence's quiet strength, cleverness of mind, and *knowing* powers were confusingly palpable to him. Stealthily using her *ethereal skills* before he offered what he was going to do or say unsettled him terribly. *"Yes, I'll go out back and get the fresh well water to go with your lunch"*; *"I know you want cornbread and snap peas with those chops for supper"*; *"Yes, I agree, I think you should go to town now for those tractor parts."*

"God almighty, Sheriff, she confounds me with those ways of hers," he'd tell me if I saw him in town. And Benevolence would tell me with a bit of a snicker, *"That ole Ezekiel Beals, he simply growls and groans back at me like some distressed animal. He gives me an unwavering stare like he is coring an apple, and with his typical scowl and resentful face, he says to me: 'What you are saying to me, girly? You best stop that smart mouth of yours or I'll—'"*

He was clearly irritated by the exactness with which she would convey his very own unspoken thoughts, but Benevolence, with her typical calm resolve, would give him her quite assured reply. *"Well, it's what you were going to tell me anyway, isn't that right, Mr. Beals?"* Ezekiel Beals's only recant to Benevolence would be his large, clenched fist pounding on the oval, oak, kitchen table, clearly exasperated with her, but he just couldn't argue further with Benevolence about the very thoughts he had been thinking and the things he wanted before he even asked for them. As much as he hated to admit it, since Beauty's passing, Ezekiel Beals had come to rely on Benevolence. They were an odd pair, but they made it work for each other.

ℰ0ℰ0ℰ0

Though I had made my way with Ezekiel Beals in the twenty-one years since my mother's passing, at an unexpected moment, my world would split apart from my present-day, and dark memories would intrude upon me while I was doing my chores. I would be transported to the gravesite funeral of my dear mama, who was just thirty-nine years old at the time of her death. Those stark memories seemed to be intractable crevices in my mind and heart, but then I'd ponder for a second that maybe everybody experiences being transported to another time in their mind about losing someone they cherished—and how I cherished my mama. Anyway, that particular memory would suddenly swoop in and hang in my mind like low-lying clouds rumbling overhead before a rainstorm. And there I'd be in my mind's eye, a scared little ten-year-old girl, trembling uncontrollably. My legs and hands twitching nervously, and Ezekiel Beals's big hand, with those thick fingers of his, wrapped around mine, clutching my little fingers so tight I thought the circulation in my fingers would stop. A collage of images were in my mind—there we were together, by that graveside. The two of us stood straight and tall, with bowed heads. Both of us wrapped in our disillusioned heartache, each for our own reasons about the loss of my mama—the sweet but tough Miss Beauty Eveline Pumpkin.

In our small but sorrowful band, the ladies from Mama's New Hope AME Church came looking respectful and solemn in their Sunday best dresses and big-brimmed hats. The honorable Judge Lucas and Sheriff Louis Francis Roulette were also standing so erect. Sheriff Louie was across from me on the other side of my mama's coffin, and he was holding his tan Stetson sheriff's hat over his chest all the while, never taking his eyes off of me. As I recall, when I happened to look up, Sheriff Louie gave me a warm smile and a gentle nod of his head—a gesture of re-assurance, I felt. It was such a brief but fleeting sense of reassurance from a caring adult who might help me. Yet, there on that dismal, autumn, Sunday afternoon, when the rain was soft with a steady mist, the sky overcast with slow-moving cumulus clouds, the dark moss hanging low from the branches of ancient sea oaks casting their shadows over a coffin not yet placed in the ground, I knew even at ten years old, that hard pressing clutch of Ezekiel Beals hand against mine *was not* because he was trying to convey to me by his touch that he was sorry that my mama had died or that his firm grasp was coming from care or concern for me—the little girl of ten years old standing beside him who just lost the only safe anchor in her life. No, I knew even then, the firm clutching grip of Ezekiel Beals at my mama's gravesite was to let me know his total and complete dominance over me would go unabashed and swift now that Mama was gone. That morning, as I half listened to the White preacher's droning, rambling words in those dreadful moments at my mama's funeral, I *knew* more than ever before, what I must now face alone. Oh, by the way, I did ask that ole Mr. Beals if the Reverend Albert from my mama's church could say a few words about Mama and he flat out told me to my face, "No!" Mr. Beals was always jealous of the abundance of love and unabated devotion Mama showed me, so he sho'nuff was not gonna abide by my request even upon her death. The reality that existed between us was bleak. There would be no balance of power now with my mama gone. Life would not be in my favor by virtue of my age, the color of my skin, his years of resentment toward me, and my complete alone-ness.

21

What I will tell you is that since my mama's death, ole Ezekiel Beals's tone toward me was always gruff and harsh, his words curt and unfeeling, his countenance superior, domineering, and demanding—and always with a permanent scowl on his face. But he never touched me in that way that girls and women, White or Black, fear from an angry, unhappy, insecure man. But ole Mr. Ezekiel did take a switch to my bottom or swing the brass buckle from his leather belt at my legs that would leave welts on my skin. Most of the time, I could outrun him. He couldn't stand that, as I would laugh to myself at my small victory. The infractions that did upset him, I thought even as a little girl, were silly and petty and certainly did not warrant any kind of punishment . . . just seemed to me that ole man liked to hear himself talk and fuss at me: I didn't secure the top on the ketchup bottle tight enough, the lid atop the corn bin for the chickens wasn't positioned just right, there were detergent flakes on the laundry room floor that needed *immediate* sweeping up, or his morning coffee was too strong. His foolish demands and reprimands upon me were seemingly endless throughout my childhood and early adolescence.

But as I got older, it all stopped! I am absolutely confident it was because of my cooking—following my mama's recipes to the letter. Well, that ole Mr. Ezekiel was as silent and still as those hot and humid airs that cover us on a Mississippi summer night. He would eat each morsel of the food I would prepare for us voraciously! I *knew* there was absolutely nothing to complain about with my cooking, and I *knew* he would surely never admit to me that he enjoyed my cooking.

ജ്ഞജ്ഞ

So, now that y'all have some back story about Sheriff Louie and me, we will come back to the afternoon that is at the crux of this story. It was a sweltering hot, and humid, Mississippi August mid-morning, not even eleven a.m. yet. I stood at the kitchen sink, slowly and methodically washing breakfast dishes left from the morning and pondering to myself what had just occurred. I felt grateful, relieved, even overjoyed, and yet wondering who would believe me about what had taken place on that day. I recalled to myself, *Ever since I was a child, the folks of Cypress Groves thought I had very peculiar ways for a little girl.* As I walked to the kitchen table, I glanced into the living room and looked pensively at Mr. Ezekiel Beals lying still and lifeless on *my* living room floor.

When I sat down at the kitchen table and gazed out the open kitchen windows, looking at the sprawling limbs from the weeping willow that had graced Ezekiel Beals's front yard since I was a little girl, the long winding gravel driveway to the house lay ahead of my vision as well. I recalled watching lots of folks come down that gravel road over the years. Those coming down the winding driveway always brought up a swirl of dust from the sandy, dry, Mississippi dirt, alerting us somebody was coming to the house. There was young Jacob Tippy, delivering groceries on the back of his John Deere tractor; Mr. Eddie, the propane man, filling up the tanks for the winter chill; Alberto's Asphalt Company delivering driveway pebbles for Mr. Beals's front yard turn-around; Miss Rita, the chicken lady, delivering a fresh batch of two dozen large eggs from her finest Dixie White hens—cause Mr. Beals only wanted the eggs from Miss Rita's Dixie Whites, although Miss Rita had more than eleven different breeds of fine cooking hens; and my mama, when she was alive, driving Mr. Beals's blue and white '58 Ford Fairlane station wagon was always the best sight, bringing those new, white, ankle socks with those pretty, little, red roses stitched on the edge of the lace from the Belk in town. Yes, the sight of my mama traveling down that dusty dirt driveway was as special as seeing the first bloom of pink dogwoods on an April day or as delicious as that first lick of a vanilla ice cream cone dipped in dark chocolate from the Dairy Queen in town.

And on that day, with Ezekiel Beals lying dead on *my* living room floor, I could hear Mama's voice in my ear — what she had told me since I was a little girl — *"And if I goes before him . . . my half will be yours, baby girl. That's right! I made sure it was official and all . . . Judge Lucas in town he wrote us up a will and all. And when that Mr. Beals is gone, why, the whole lot of it is yours."* She would further emphasize to me, *"All of it Benevolence Mae. The house, the land; it's all written up tight as a tick in the will in my chest-a-draws. I made sure of that!"* My mama would remind me now and then that it was to be *my* house, *my* kitchen, and *my* land. This fact always consoled me on those dark days when I endured the sting from the back of his hand on my cheek, or the lash of the wood switch, or the brass belt buckle swatted across my bottom.

ഇഇഇ

In those adrenaline-filled moments, I heard Benevolence's calm, smooth, silky southern drawl with her articulate words lingering in my head. Trying to grasp what I just heard and, as unsettling as it was, I had quickly begun to formulate questions in my mind and was seconds away from asking Benevolence, when there it was — those special *knowing ways* of hers. Benevolence quickly and assuredly answered the very questions I was about to ask her but had not as yet even spoken aloud.

"Yes, I'm all right and yes, Sheriff Louie, that ole man is dead on *my* living room floor!"

"Did I hear you right, Benevolence, about Ezekiel Beals? Did you say he was dead on the living room floor?"

"Yes, Sheriff, that's sho'nuff what I said."

Although I was filled with urgency to get out to Ezekiel's place, I had immediately noted two things Benevolence had said. First, Benevolence had done what she always did ever since she was a little girl—*knowing* folks' minds and thoughts and answering their questions even before they asked them, and second, she emphasized that ole Ezekiel Beals was dead on *"her"* living room floor! She had laid claim to Ezekiel's home!

"And you sure you are all right, Benevolence?" I asked with concern.

Almost exasperated with my question, Benevolence continued with more directness and a bit of impatience, "Yes, Sheriff Louie, I am fine . . . just as fine as a fresh spring morning, and yes, sir, as I said to you, Mr. Beals, he is dead . . . he is as dead as that ole gray-haired Oscar buried out back in Mama's vegetable-rose garden when he gasped and spit out his last hairball. I am looking at ole Mr. Beals right now. Yeah, he's dead all right and just-a bleedin' away on *my* living room floor. Guess you should come take a look-see."

I was usually steady and calm when receiving calls like these, having been the sheriff in Jackson County for the past nineteen years. After all, I had seen my share of all kinds of death in the Gulf coast of Mississippi—some by an immediate, impulsive, and violent act; some strange and peculiar and unexplained; some swift and unexpected—but this time more than others, I was particularly unsettled because it was Benevolence Mae calling me about a death. Though I expected such disturbing phone calls as appropriate to the office held by a sheriff, I never thought the next one that arrived at my office would be from Miss Beauty's daughter. I knew despite all these years of being under Ezekiel's thumb, Benevolence always made do with ole Ezekiel. As I was fond of Benevolence and always protective of her—checking on her from time to time out at Ezekiel's place, since Miss Beauty's passing—I was particularly concerned for her considering the circumstances she had just informed me of.

"I'm on my way, Benevolence. Now you stay put and don't move anything. I'll be there in about forty minutes. I need to pick up JW first, though."

"Of course, Sheriff Louie, I'm *not* going anywhere, I'm *not* going to move anything. And sure, bring on that Yankee-boy deputy of yours." Benevolence answered me with a steadied voice, perturbed by my requests. Benevolence continued: "First of all, Sheriff Louie, I got supper cooking on the stove simmering on a low boil; got some big ole prawns from the Texas gulf and tasty crawfish just caught fresh from Stewart's Fishmart, a nice plumb mallet too, my honey-cured ham—hot just out of the oven—beets from Mama's garden that I picked months ago just popped on top of them, and my special cornbread with roasted pecans, chopped onions, celery and kernels of that white sweet corn in the oven as we speak. No, sir, I won't be going anywhere. Now, y'all come on, take a look at this, and then maybe you and that Yankee-boy deputy of yours will join me for an early supper. And yes, all the while I'm telling ya about supper, Sheriff Louie, I am still looking over at Mr. Ezekiel Beals's crumpled-up lifeless body on *my* living room floor."

On the way to pick up JW, I was trying to put together what Benevolence just told me, and that "Yankee-boy deputy" Benevolence was talking about is J. W. Riley. It's obvious he is NOT Southern. The locals, both Black and White, refer to him as "that tall, lanky, fast-talking, peach-fuzz, pushy, White Yankee-boy." JW was easier to say than "Julius Winston" and what he "preferred," as he informed me when he first applied for the job. I told him, *"Well, son, if you even get the job, my first order of business will be calling you JW because that's what I "prefer" to call you!"* JW did end up being my newly appointed deputy because no one else applied for the job, but JW never knew that.

And what brought this Yankee-boy south? It was JW's own self-professed desire to *"Get out of the noisy and congested New York City."* His great Aunt Tilly, who was a born and bred Alabama "Roll Tide" Southern gal, had a palatial, white-columned, antebellum, colonial house in Tuscaloosa, with plenty of empty rooms in it, which she occupied by herself and could use the company of her great nephew—*Julius Winston.* So, JW stayed rent-free as he finished his BA degree in criminal justice at the University of Alabama.

JW made his way to me due to the ad I placed in our local newspaper, the Cyprus Grove Sentinel, *"In need of a deputy with or without prior experience."* JW fit the latter part of the job description to the *T!*

ಬಬಬ

27

And so, our day began.

Driving down Ezekiel's long gravel driveway, dust clouds circled behind me on the long dirt road leading to the three-story house on the marsh. I parked in the front yard under the weeping willow tree that stood right beside the flagpole where that ole Dixie flag, now tattered and frayed from years of flapping in the wind, lay limp and motionless in the hot and humid August afternoon's blazing sun.

I saw Benevolence staring at us through her open kitchen window. I turned off my truck, a pretty beat-up Ford Ranger with dents and dings, and long key scratches on both doors by who knows what kids around town. I don't like driving the sheriff's patrol car, too officious for these parts of the Delta in Jackson County, and I learned years ago folks tended to be on guard when they saw that patrol car coming.

I opened the truck door and slowly swung my six-foot, three-inch frame out of the driver's side of the truck . . . not always an easy task, and more so lately. I could hear myself moan and groan. I have had a permanent limp in my right leg ever since the Malcolm brothers shot at me and shattered my right kneecap when I was trying to break up their moonshine still, and it's left me *euuuing* and *ahhing* when I try to lift or bend down my right knee. So, the mounting scar tissue tightening around my kneecap and the increasing arthritis on the tendons surrounding the right knee has now left me with a constant chronic ache; also the reason for hiring a young, more agile, deputy. I've hated to admit it to myself, but I can't walk or run like I used to cause of my right knee.

ဆဆဆ

I watched out my open kitchen window as Sheriff Louie limped toward the kitchen screen door and that young Yankee deputy of his jumped out of the passenger side of the truck like an eager puppy raring to run around the yard, helter-skelter, to catch his own tail. Deputy Riley slammed the truck door behind himself and strode toward my house like he had the full force of the archangels behind him. I thought to myself, *Yes, he's just a chomping at the bit to find a murderess here . . . he's probably already made up his mind about me—sho'nuff, that Yankee boy has.*

As Sheriff Louie ambled over to my kitchen screen door, I could hear his boots crunching on the little pebble rocks of the dirt driveway under the souls of his boots—a familiar sound I so often dreaded for many years of my childhood after Mama died. I knew Sheriff Louie would gather the dust of Mississippi's red, sandy clay on the tips of his black leather, well-worn, scuffed-up Lucchese cowboy boots—a cold, chilling memory of that all-too-familiar gruff, raspy voice popped in my mind while, in my heart, I was surprised, because I could feel a cauldron of fear bubbling up in me like I was that little eleven-year-old girl again. It would be ole Ezekiel's shoes I would have to scrub off the red, sandy clay and then polish and he would admonish me, *"Better get these shoes cleaned up like new or I'll be taking you back behind the barn and switch your behind, girlie."*

That dreadful memory was interrupted by Sheriff Louie knocking on the wood frame of my faded, green, kitchen screen door with its paint peeling and chipped from the long summer days of the blistering Mississippi heat. Before he could call my name, I called out to him, "Sheriff, y'all come on in . . ."

Sheriff Louie opened the squeaky ole kitchen screen

door slowly, with Deputy J. W. Riley dutifully following closely behind, letting the screen door shut abruptly behind him. I didn't flinch, nor turn around toward them, as I heard the kitchen screen door close with its customary sounds of creaking, weatherworn hinges from years of wear and tear and neglect.

It too was a familiar yet unwelcome sound from my childhood—with the sound of the slamming kitchen screen door and creaking hinges, I was transported quickly to another old, bleak, dark memory that draped over me like an ill-fitting shawl. I couldn't shut down the stream of memories. My thoughts carried me to those harrowing moments when, if there was enough time as *he* opened the kitchen screen door and before *he* got a glance at me, Mama's gaze would land on me with urgency and, with one hand behind her back, shoo me off, while at the same time under her breath softly saying with care, *"Scoot, little girl, scoot quick like the wind under an angel's wings!"*

I would hustle as quickly as my little feet in my Buster Brown shoes could carry me out of the kitchen into the living room parlor, down the long hallway that led to another screen door onto a back porch in the rear of the house, and scurry down three steps that poured into my mother's sprawling vegetable and rose garden. Deep exhales always came afterward, having entered the safety and peace of being far away from *him*.

Thankfully, that memory too was halted by Sheriff Louie's declaration of care and his usual pragmatism, yet his tone was laced with confusion and surprise at the sight he was gazing upon.

"Hmm, my goodness, Benevolence, this is quite a scene."

And there he was, just like I had told Sheriff Louie over

the phone, face down right in the middle of the living room floor, legs together and his body curved a bit with his arms underneath his stomach. There lay Mr. Ezekiel Beals, lifeless in a pool of coagulating, maroon-colored blood. I turned my head and watched Sheriff Louie walk into the living room and kneel down slowly on his left knee, so as to not put any pressure on his bad knee. He took a pulse from Ezekiel's neck, and then Sheriff Louie hoisted himself upright on the edge of the yellow-and-gray-speckled Formica laundry room table I had moved into the living room to cut rose thorns off of the beautiful, warm, red floribunda roses my mama had planted in her vegetable garden. Upon inspecting ole Mr. Beals, Sheriff Louie walked into the kitchen and leaned his large-framed body against the kitchen counter. He first looked out the open window over the kitchen sink, then at me still standing at the kitchen sink *slowly* washing the morning's breakfast dishes—just the same way my mama used to each morning.

The silence among the three of us was only punctuated by the whoosh of running water from the kitchen faucet. I interrupted the silence and spoke with some irritation, looking over my shoulder to Sheriff Louie.

"Well, Sheriff Louie, best be getting about your sheriffing duties. I got to get on to my day's schedule and begin preparing for my early supper, just like Mama would do."

༄༄༄

With my white, cotton handkerchief in hand, I wiped the sweat from my brow as beads of perspiration gathered around the top of my lip in the humid heat that crept through the open kitchen window into the non-air-conditioned house of Ezekiel Beals . . . or, *now*, Benevolence's home. I heard the steadfast resolve in Benevolence's voice but most of all I heard the melancholy in her tone, and I *felt* her yearning for someone familiar, so much so, that I got a deep pain in my own gut at that moment. No matter the time that passed, it was that same edge of melancholy that followed me . . . the same way I felt missing my sweet Clare Claudette.

"I see, Benevolence, Ezekiel sho'nuff is dead right here on that living room floor just like you told me! Yes, I know you have your day's schedule to attend to, Benevolence. But I do have to find out what happened here." I paused and peered solemnly at Benevolence and then again at Ezekiel Beals's still-lifeless body. I continued, "Well, I do need to hear from you, Benevolence, *everything* that happened here in this house."

Benevolence had finished washing her breakfast dishes and turned toward me with a determined gaze, answering me swiftly and with exasperation. "What do you mean?! You mean about that ole cantankerous, mean bear of a man? Well, *he's dead.* I mean look at him, Sheriff Louie . . . that is a dead man right there, just as I told you! And I know what you are thinking, Sheriff Louie. But first, well, it wouldn't be just me that couldn't stand that ole man." Benevolence's words seared with matter-of-fact sharpness as she peered directly at the man and nodded to the motionless body on the living room floor before them.

"Dead all right, he is, Sheriff Louie. Like I told you, dead on *my* living room floor, that ole man is!" I noted she quickly claimed ownership of the home of her mother and Ezekiel.

Benevolence was right. I knew Ezekiel Beals had few friends in his lifetime and had just as many folks, Black or

White, who disliked him for any number of reasons—his greedy business practices, his impetuous short temper, his bad manners, his hypocritical biases and prejudices, and his plain, overall unpleasant nature. The only person who could ever tame him was Miss Beauty Pumpkin, and the only person who could ever put up with him was Miss Beauty Pumpkin. Most people thought Beauty Pumpkin had put a potion in his morning coffee years ago and that's what enchanted him in her presence. I knew Ezekiel treated Benevolence the same way Ezekiel treated everyone, and most likely worse—at least, when Beauty wasn't around to protect her. Ezekiel Beals knew he would never rise to the level of importance in Beauty's eyes or heart, as Miss Beauty would always refer to Benevolence as her *"precious, little, baby girl."* He knew he had to tolerate that. Obviously, the two of them had an understanding between themselves. Everybody knew Ezekiel had to play quite a balancing act of restraint between what he really thought and felt toward Benevolence and what he felt for Beauty. At least, most times Benevolence was safe when Miss Beauty was nearby.

ℰℭℰℭℰℭ

Before I go about telling you how Benevolence explained to me the demise of Ezekiel, it's important you also know something about Mr. Ezekiel Beals of Cyprus Groves, Mississippi. The land Ezekiel held had been in the Beals family for generations since the 1800s—cotton fields mostly—and he inherited it from his father as did his father from his father, and so on. Ezekiel Beals felt a strong bond to his land and rightfully so, after centuries of ownership, but Ezekiel was not a financially wealthy man by any means. He was comfortable money-wise, and he got by like most "land-rich" folks in the Marsh did. More importantly, Ezekiel Beals was no stranger to me as sheriff of Cypress Groves. Ezekiel was one of the most vocal of Cypress Grove's White citizens to my sheriff's office. If I didn't receive a phone call or two almost every week from Ezekiel, I'm here to tell you I sho'nuff received a call from him every other week complaining about something . . . usually petty, usually minor, usually racist and prejudiced, and always with the same veiled threat attached, *"Now, you know the sheriff's job is voted in by its citizens of this county, so I expect to get my vote's worth of your attention, Sheriff Roulette, you hear me! I don't know how they do things in that big sinful city of New Or-leens where you come from, but down here in the Mississippi-Delta, our public servants do whatever we say and whenever we say it. So, you get your New Or-leens butt over here, and you tell that skinny, Yankee deputy of yourn to hang back. I don't need no questions from him when y'all get here,"* or *"Sheriff, you come on down here today to my farm and see what those negro boys of Ms. Jessie's did to my hen house again. I told you too many times about those young boys messing with my hens. You gotta go on and arrest them kids. Those negro kids gonna end up in jail anyway, I don't care how young they are,"* or *"Sheriff Roulette, somebody done let the air out of my John Deere tires again, most likely some unattended Blacky young'uns of Miss Jessie's. You come down here to my place and investigate this now!"* And the list of requests from Ezekiel Beals would go on and on and had so for years!

However, I sho'nuff didn't wish ole Ezekiel any harm, despite his cold, uncaring, and blatantly biased, racist nature. As troublesome and difficult as Ezekiel was, I also knew Ezekiel was simply trying to voice his right of ownership to *his* land, *his* property, and I knew any White Southerner didn't like anybody coming on *their* land uninvited and unannounced, and certainly not Black kids. Yet, I also knew there were plenty of White families with mischievous kids of their own that lived around the edges of Ezekiel's land . . . and, usually more often than not, after I investigated Ezekiel's request, typically both the Black and White kids that lived around Ezekiel's farm were joining in together, enjoying causing havoc on Ezekiel's land. However, Ezekiel Beals would never hear just as many White kids were to blame for the mischief caused to Ezekiel's hen house or to his flattened John Deere tractor tires as were the Black kids.

Ezekiel Beals was a sullen and angry man for most of his life. He once had prestige in the county, but when it became clear he had "taken up with that Miss Beauty," he was shunned and laughed at behind his back. Ezekiel knew this but it didn't stop him from having Miss Beauty with him when he drove into town to shop at Abbot's Market or stop by Wilson's hardware store. Ezekiel was simply tolerated by the White folks in the community and, worst of all to him, he knew he was looked down on by the Black folks of Cypress Groves. For a Mississippi Southerner like Ezekiel Beals, that was the most damaging to his self-righteous prejudiced ego.

ജ്ഞജ്ഞ

Benevolence had come to sit down at the oval, oak kitchen table that Ezekiel had made years ago when Miss Beauty was alive. She was looking out her kitchen windows that spanned the back of the house and overlooked large green pasture land. Benevolence was watching a large expanse of slow-moving, feathery, white clouds against a blanket of azure blue sky, and under her breath, half speaking to me and half speaking to somewhere far off beyond the Mississippi horizon, she said, "Yes, feels hot today and . . . thick humid today, isn't it? I can feel it in my bones, I can hear it, the sound of vibrating hot air here in *my* kitchen, even now . . . in *my* kitchen. Oh, yeah, Sheriff Louie, that ole Mr. Beals is gone to someplace beyond for the likes of him. Yes, that sorry-sight-of-a-White man is sho'nuff dead and gone back to the darkness where he came from!"

Then, Benevolence glared at me and JW with those crystalline blue eyes of hers, her hands folded on the table, continued with an uncharacteristic edge of annoyance in her tone, "Now, y'all go do whatever you have to do, but you both are going to have to excuse me. I'm going to look after my supper and get my cornbread out of the oven! And when you're finished in there," Benevolence gestured to the living room, "plenty for y'all both too, if you're hungry." Benevolence took a quick glance at the lifeless body of Ezekiel Beals on her living room floor, gave me a steely gaze as she got up from the kitchen table, and walked over to her oven, bent down, and opened the oven door to a wafting luscious fragrance of her golden cake of cornbread.

"Oh, can't y'all just smell my sweet cornbread? My goodness, just like Mama's!" Benevolence said to herself with great pleasure.

"Well, all right, Benevolence, while you take care of supper, Deputy Riley and I are going to look around a bit, okay? And at supper, you *will* tell me exactly what happened here." For the first time since I arrived, I was more firm with Benevolence.

Benevolence grunted with emphasis, "Hmph, Sheriff Louie, well . . . y'all two go do whatever you need to do.

Y'all going to do it anyway, so don't know why you ask me if it's okay? No need to ask my permission, you being the sheriff and all, examining the scene of an accident or . . . *something*." Glancing ever so slightly to the left of her shoulder, Benevolence echoed softly and lovingly, "Now, look at that, will ya, Mama? This cornbread is just perfect now, just the right golden yellow like you always made . . . just like you taught me."

JW looked quizzically at me, and I noted he caught that Benevolence had called Ezekiel's death "an accident or something." I *knew* the young deputy was about to speak to me when I interrupted him, on the verge of his open mouth, and with an edge of my own impatience in my voice, I ordered my young deputy before entering the living room, "I heard her, JW, and before you do anything else, I want you to call the medical examiner and tell him to get to Ezekiel Beals's place ASAP."

Under his breath, I heard JW murmur, "Doubt it's an *accident*, and she doesn't seem rattled by all of this. If you ask me, Miss Benevolence kinda got an attitude about it all . . ." JW let his gaze fall to the dead body on the living room floor and then toward Benevolence and me alike, "Talking to herself like that," JW said to me with in-experience about inexplicable things.

I shook myself a bit as I was aware of the *"feeling"* that had come over me since I entered the kitchen . . . that familiar *feeling* . . . remote and distant like I wasn't in the present. The feeling always came when *a "knowing"* came upon me. *Perceiving* something from beyond—an absolute knowing and feeling without doubt or question. It resonates deep in my gut 'bout someone or something present before me, or something 'bout to happen without having substantial, evidential facts to support the experience. The same way I *knew* about Charles Louis Gerard when I was ten years old and so many other times in my life . . . that *knowing*—that *sensing* without *question or doubt!* In this case, I *knew* since JW and I had arrived that something or someone was here, surrounding the three of us. For me, my first clue was the need to inhale deeply as if my breath had been momentarily taken from me, and I had to gasp for air and then the physical *knowing* passed quickly. In this case, I *knew* we three were not alone, and I was sure it was her with us . . . it was Miss Beauty with us for sure.

As JW and I walked into the living room, I greeted Miss Beauty out loud, softly and respectfully, "Hey, Miss Beauty."

JW turned and looked at me oddly, unaware of such a phenomenon, and asked, "What did you say, Sheriff?"

"Nothing, JW. Just collect this broken glass for evidence," I said as I pointed to the broken glass on the floor below the fireplace mantel, "and when you're done with that, make sure you tape off the entire living room . . . it's a crime scene."

JW quickly put on the latex gloves and pulled out evidence bags he had stuffed in his back pocket, poised to gather evidence lurking in the rooms he and I were about to investigate. At all times, despite what I *knew* and had already *seen*, I still employed my usual crime investigation acumen sound principles of crime investigation. First, putting on my latex gloves so as not to contaminate any other fingerprints around the room, and then stopping and slowly surveying the room clockwise, looking for messages hidden in ordinary places that others would easily overlook. Asking myself what is out of the ordinary here? What mistakes might the perpetrator have made while hastily leaving the scene of the crime? What is the "unique signature" that this perpetrator left behind to taunt us or show his or her arrogance?

But despite the usual investigative procedures that needed to occur, there it was—the undeniable scent overpowering me. A wonderful, sweet-yet-subtle scent *maybe like gardenias or magnolias . . . no, that's too sweet . . . lilacs or quince, maybe—no not the season for those. It's softer. Ah, yeah, it's honeysuckle and rose. That's it . . . heavy here in this room. Sho'nuff is honeysuckle and the drop-dead red floribunda rose that Miss Beauty was known to grow in her vegetable garden.*

I smiled to myself and tucked that *knowing* away momentarily. Then, JW and I continued glancing at the obvious before us—living room chairs strewn on the floor, a small side table turned over and all the shattered glass scattered around the living room. I heard my own thoughts, *All right, Miss Beauty, what is it you want me to know here?*

I touched the seat of the red, rose-patterned, cloth lounge chair. *This was Miss Beauty's sitting chair. It's water soaked. The scent of honeysuckle and red roses are still lingering in my nose. What is it, Miss Beauty?* I noticed a small picture frame with its glass shattered and broken into pieces along with two mason jars broken and littered on the hardwood floor. With the toe of my right boot shuffled gently through some of the pieces of glass, I noticed a few were blood stained.

"JW, be sure and pick these up and place them in the evidence bag," I told him as I looked at my boot tip.

Following my directions dutifully, JW diligently and carefully picked up the blood-stained pieces of glass with his latex-covered fingertips and placed them in an evidence bag.

Pictures that once neatly graced the fireplace mantel were now strewn on the living room floor with the glass cracked and some glass, jagged edges still inside their frames. I had to place my right hand alongside the brick fireplace to steady myself, about to bend down to the broken glass on the floor. As I slowly bent down, I was aware of the chronic ache in my right knee and the cracking sound it always made when I had to bend down on it. *Damn, I'm not as agile as I once had been . . . so aggravating,* I thought.

I grabbed the handkerchief from my back pocket . . . not always trusting those thin, latex gloves that we were supposed to use at crime scenes and carefully picked up a large, mahogany frame, some of the broken glass was still in its frame, and there was a Polaroid picture. There she was as I always remembered her—Miss Beauty Pumpkin—a lovely, dark-skinned, tall, young woman standing erect, looking ever graceful as always, yet with that familiar melancholic gaze starring to some far-off place beyond the Mississippi horizon. Memories flooded the moment for me. Despite all, Miss Beauty always held a kind expression on her face and was quick to give a gentle smile to any passerby she saw in town and especially when she greeted me in town. And those of us who cared to notice, and there were some in Cypress Groves, Mississippi, both Black and White, knew behind Beauty Pumpkin's typically jovial nature, her kind smile, and her steadfast graciousness to *anyone* she met whether it was reciprocated or not, in her luminous light blue eyes existed a constant sadness—an emptiness was revealed. And what I *saw* and *knew* in her Spirit was an ever-present, swirling energy of resignation because she was trapped by the life Natchez had directed her to take on and abiding by his wishes as she knew he was right—a better life for her and Benevolence would be had with Ezekiel Beals in spite of his all-too-often cold, miasmatic presence.

I had always *felt* and *saw* in Miss Beauty something similar in myself . . . that all too familiar concoction of sadness, resignation, and loss lingering just on the edge of a smile. Although the loves of our lives were long since gone, the deep magnetic love we had for our soulmates and them for us—the happiness we felt in their presence—that mutual cherished passionate compelling love was *always* present in our hearts no matter the time or distance that separated us now from their earthly presence.

And in those moments that passed in the living room, I was lost in what I saw in the broken glass before me—that kind of lost love Miss Beauty had for Natchez and I for Clare Claudette and those broken lives staring back at me . . . Beauty, Benevolence, and even ole Ezekiel. I reminded myself and spoke to Miss Beauty through my thoughts. *Hey, Miss Beauty, all those seemingly fine, Southern, church-going ladies, Black and White alike, with their endless whispering gossiping behind your back passing judgment on you and Ezekiel. Why, they believe y'all were "living in sin and damned to hell lying down together being a White man with a Black woman!" We are a bit more liberal in New Or-leens, you know . . . and truer still, most of these folks down here on the Marsh think you placed a potion in Ezekiel's morning coffee and that's what had him enchanted in your presence!*

I chuckled to myself under my breath.

ഈഈഈ

I gingerly held in my hands the picture frame with its cracked and broken glass and, there standing beside Miss

Beauty, was Ezekiel Beals grinning from ear to ear with his arm clumsily around Miss Beauty. His face held a boastful pride like he had bagged a buck in open deer season. And behind them both was a small child sitting on a wooden swing that hung from a large, out-stretched, gnarly limb of that weeping willow tree that could be seen from the kitchen window. And through the cracked glass, I saw a gently round, little, light-skinned Black girl, wearing a pretty, multicolored, sleeveless sundress with her shiny, brown-leather, lace-up shoes, barely touching the ground, and those delicate, white, lacey ankle socks with little, pink roses stitched on the edges of the lace tucked neatly in her shoes. There she was, proud as could be, Benevolence Pumpkin, with an innocent big smile on her face, holding tenderly in her little coco brown arms, a large, gray and white, fury kitten that she had named Oscar. *Sho'nuff, a sad day for some of us in Cypress Groves when you died, but most of all a sad and treacherous day for you, Benevolence, you that little ten-year-old girl who was left behind,* the thought whispered in my mind.

Suddenly again, I was sharply distracted from my thoughts, *Lord, I declare heavier now . . . honeysuckle and rose.* A slight smile came across my face, and I chuckled out loud and said under my breath, "All right then, Miss Beauty, you're here. What do you want me to know? To see? You lead and I'll follow." I smiled to myself.

"What did you say, Sheriff?" JW asked me eagerly as he continued to survey the dining and living room, yet patiently waiting sentry for further directions.

"Nothing, nothing, JW. Keep looking for anything un-usual. Look for something in a different way . . . look for what we would see . . . not what *is* here," I responded briskly, yet always determined to guide JW. I noticed more often than not these days, I was short-tempered with JW.

Good Lord, not his fault, I thought. *I'm just tired . . . tired of bearing witness to people's pain, tired of people's disregard for human life. I believe I'm at the point of being more interested in catching fish over criminals. I have to keep grooming JW to maybe . . . someday, if he can prove himself competent enough, to take my place. Though, not that JW is showing much competence anytime soon. He'd sho'nuff have to win the confidence of folks down here in Mississippi for them to vote in a young guy from up North as sheriff! Good Lord, that's gonna be a tall order!*

ഇരുന്ന

"If you two done with that, you want to eat with me?" Benevolence called out from the kitchen.

Unable to contain himself, young deputy Riley responded quickly and clearly. "Sure," and he bolted for the kitchen. I knew he'd been distracted throughout our investigation by the mouthwatering smells of Benevolence Pumpkin's golden cornbread and honey-cured ham. He was caught up in the magical spell of her Southern culinary delights. *Those aromas caught me too!* I watched as JW reached the kitchen. He was jolted for a moment, not because Ezekiel Beals's body was lying between the threshold of the living room and the kitchen entryway, or because he had placed the crime tape across the living room entryway but because of what he saw before him. I knew Benevolence had set the kitchen table for three just the way Miss Beauty would have taught her. Benevolence would have Miss Beauty's fine china supper dishes, crisp white linen napkins, glistening heirloom silverware, and etched stemmed glasses filled with sun-brewed tea, fresh lemon slices, and sprigs of peppermint leaves floating on ice cubes. A tall, slender, gleaming, etched glass vase filled bountifully with fresh flowers from Miss

Beauty's garden held her two favorite types of roses: fresh cut, velvety deep, scarlet *drop dead red* floribunda roses and her soft, blush pink roses. They adorned the center of the oval, oak kitchen table.

"My goodness, Miss Pumpkin, you certainly set a beautiful table," I heard JW respond to Benevolence.

"Humph . . . you Yankee-boys think we folks down South don't know how to set a table for a proper supper!" Benevolence never held back what she really thought, and I chuckled to myself, hearing her put JW in his place.

"Come on in here, son, and sit down before this food gets cold. You can leave the investigating to Sheriff Louie for the time being. He's pretty good at it by now, you know. Best leave the eating to us," Benevolence said with authority, as the young JW complied with great gusto, bending underneath the crime tape and stepping into the kitchen, pulling back a chair from the kitchen table, his eyes beaming with delight at the feast spread before him.

And JW took a big mouthful of Benevolence's scrumptious honey-baked ham, pole beans, and her famous cornbread slathered in melting butter, and with his mouth full, he exclaimed to Benevolence, "Oh, my God, Miss Benevolence, this is incredibly delicious! 'Good Lord!' as you people say down here. I've never quite tasted anything any better!"

"Humph, well we know that's right, boy." Benevolence chuckled out loud as she looked at her plate. "I'm sure as the sun's gonna rise tomorrow y'all don't have anything like this spread up Yankee way, and, young Deputy, you might want to think about *not* saying something like 'you people' when ya talking directly to us . . . we are proud Mississippi Delta folks . . . Black or White . . . you're having a hard enough time as it is with us Delta folks knowing you from New York City and all." Benevolence offered JW with a firm kindness.

JW responded respectfully. "Oh, yes, ma'am I appreciate you giving me that suggestion. My auntie in Alabama tells me all the time I have a lot to learn about living in the South."

"Well, she is right, young Deputy, best you listen to your auntie more often."

I almost couldn't bear it because I know how delectable Benevolence's food is. From the living room, I called to JW, "Best put that fork down now, and before you put anything else in your mouth, get yourself back in here and finish dusting for fingerprints."

"Ah, yes, sir, right away, Sheriff," JW responded contritely and dutifully, although clearly disappointed at having to be torn away from Benevolence's epicurean delights she had placed before him.

I continued to comb the hardwood floors for anything unusual. Benevolence called again from the kitchen, "Well, if you two aren't going to join me, sho'nuff not going to let any of this get cold." Benevolence sat herself down at the kitchen table set for three and began to enjoy her supper. In a matter of seconds, Benevolence felt my presence at the living room doorway and without looking up, she questioned me despite already *knowing* what I was going to ask.

"Yes, you want something, Sheriff Louie?" weaving her fork around the pole beans on her plate.

৪০৪০৪০

I knew the rule of law and investigative procedure must lead me to consider Benevolence as a suspect in the demise of Ezekiel Beals, but then again I *knew* something greater and mystical had happened here beyond stored-up human emotions of mutual resentment and dislike, as certainly there were lots of years of discontent between the two of them. I stepped over Ezekiel's body and sat down with Benevolence at the oval, oak kitchen table and reached for the glass of cold tea set before my place. I ran my fingers over the sweat beads on the chilled glass and quenched my thirst from the stifling heat with a sip of the refreshing tea flavored with fresh lemon and peppermint. Benevolence cut me a big square of her moist golden cornbread slathered with a big ole slab of butter. She placed it on my plate beside a generous slice of the thick honey-cured ham steak, with a scoop of fresh Texas prawns and crawfish, a heaping spoonful of her baby limas and pickled beets, and a hearty helping of cinnamon-spice apple sauce stewed from the apples picked off the old Honeycrisp apple tree in the backyard beside Miss Beauty's vegetable-rose garden. I had called to JW that once he had finished in the living room to come join us and finish his meal, knowing I had torn him away earlier from Benevolence's mouth-watering wonderous culinary spread.

Leaning back on the kitchen chair, I settled in with a few bites and then asked with a matter-of-fact tone, "All right, Benevolence, now tell us everything that happened here as you best recall."

Picking up the crisp white linen napkin from her lap and gracefully wiping her mouth, Benevolence spoke with a punctuated decisiveness, yet in a low and drifting manner.

"Well, all right, Sheriff. I know you have to know something about all of this,"—Benevolence waved a hand toward the living room in disarray and toward Ezekiel's lifeless body—"and about him. It happened like this. I was out in Mama's vegetable-rose garden, gathering my pole beans when I heard it."

Quickly swallowing the food I was enjoying, I asked, "Heard what, Benevolence?"

Benevolence responded soberly, "I heard my Salamagonya just squealing her little heart to high heaven from inside the house. I dropped the pole beans I had gathered up in my apron and ran into the house to see what all the raucous was about. There he was, just a cussing up a storm and running around the dining room table like some madman, tossing my living room chairs all about and a running after that little piglet. The two of them cut corners here and there around the dining room table then into the living room, his hands and arms just a flying this-way-and-that and knocking down everything in his way and my Lord! Sheriff, that ole Ezekiel was holding a butcher knife, swearing to slit her throat!"

Benevolence paused and then looked at me intently.

"Well, you know as well as I, Sheriff, nobody gonna catch a little pig in fear of the butcher's knife . . . plus, that man got so fat over the years, and with that bad, ole, dried-up, bitter, worn-out heart of his, well, he couldn't catch a snake slowly slithering across the ground in the noonday sun. So, I dashed quickly in front of him and we were almost touching each other's chests, I was so close to him . . . I could feel his heart racing inside his chest. I stood there, tall and straight, with my hands on my hips, and I shouted at him—yes, my voice thundered to holy heaven at that ole man for the first time in my life. I don't know what came over me, but I told him to put that knife down, and he best not touch a hair on that little piglet's head **OR ELSE**! My goodness, at that moment I thought, *Nobody's gonna hurt that defenseless little pig*, and somewhere deep inside me, that little girl that had been buried down for so many years had yelled for freedom.

Then, clear as a bell, I heard my mama's voice, loud and plain as you sitting across from me now . . . yes! She spoke to me, Sheriff Louie, she did. *'Now, little baby girl, that ole man's just a scared ole weak bully, he is. His heart always been all clogged up with malice and bitterness and prejudice, and even more so since I'm gone. Now's the time, baby girl . . . you let him know who's boss.'* Sheriff Louie, that's what she told me, and I did just that. I let him know who was boss! I knew Mama was right."

Thoughtfully, Benevolence continued to share with me how the tussel in the living room between she and Ezekiel came to a crescendo. Quite notable to me, she did so with a tone of optimism, pride, and finality in her voice.

"Well, I could see in his eyes they were quivering, and he was scared of me at that moment. So I just leaned in more and grabbed that butcher knife right out of his hand. He tried to struggle with me for just a wink of a second, but he felt my power stronger than his, and to his surprise, he let go of his grip on that butcher knife. I gently took it from him like he was some child scolded for getting caught with his hand in the cookie jar. I knew he saw it in my eyes. He knew at that moment I held *all* the power. For the first time in my life, in those chilling moments, I saw fear in the eyes of Ezekiel Beals. Just like the story Mama told me about the little bunny that outsmarted the big mean ole bear. Yes, sir, I knew right then I didn't have to run no more to escape Ezekiel Beals's cold clutches; didn't have to take his heartless orders; his harsh words ordering me to do *this* and *that*; didn't have to bear his scornful scowling no more. No, he and I both knew at that moment, I held all the power. And then, of course, there was that familiar sweet scent of honeysuckle and roses hovering around the both of us . . . and you and I know who that was, Sheriff, don't you?!"

JW was spellbound as he continued to listen intently to Benevolence, and with my *knowing*, it was clear to me that Miss Beauty had crossed the veil; presented herself in all her angelic form, and was right there guiding Benevolence through the whole episode with Ezekiel.

Benevolence stopped and took a glass of cold water to her lips and continued . . .

"Well, I picked up little Salamagonya, squealing all hunched up in a corner in the living room and scared out of her little ringlet tail, giving her a hug and reassuring her nobody was going to make bacon out of her. I let her out the screen door off of the living room with him standing in the middle of living room frozen-like, the color just left his face and he was as white as chalk, though both of us still held cold, dueling stares. But that old man, right then and there, sho'nuff just gave up. I walked back into the kitchen, put the butcher knife back in the knife drawer, and went back outside to Mama's vegetable garden to gather up those pole beans I let spill out of my apron. Right then and there, in those moments, sho'nuff, Sheriff Louie, I knew it was all over . . . relieved as a feeling of lightness came over me for the first time in my life since Mama's death because I knew the power had shifted in my favor."

As mesmerizing as it was with what Benevolence had shared with us, I knew I had to get the facts right for the record of what had transpired that day, and most of all, for Benevolence's sake.

"Benevolence, you said you told Ezekiel he needed to leave Salamagonya alone *'or else.'* Or else what would you have done?"

"Well, Sheriff Louie, I knew it would have been him or her, and sho'nuff wasn't gonna be my little Salamagonya. Yes, I know how that sounds. Don't really know what I would have done but those words just came out of my mouth. I don't believe they were even my words—you know, they came from someone else." Benevolence gave me a piercing gaze and said quietly and hushed, "You know she was beside me whispering in my ear. Like she was standing beside me telling me what to do and say . . ."

Benevolence looked directly at me, and I *knew*—I understood.

"And like I said, Sheriff Louie. I smelled sweet honeysuckle and rose all the while as I stood in front of Ezekiel, squaring off with him eye-to-eye. Yes, honeysuckle and rose . . . a fragrance *we* won't forget. The scent of Mama soon homeward turning but not until her business here was done. She was standing beside me the whole time, sheltering me and surrounding me with her sweet scent of honeysuckle and roses." Benevolence trailed off in a quiet, hushed tone, looking at me with soft eyes aware of the *knowing ways* we both shared.

I don't question such things. The transcendent phenomena don't perplex my earthly rational nature. Having benefited from my own French Cajun grand-mère Catalina, she told me years before, *"Mon petit amour, you have the knowing gifts, they will come easily and often unexpectedly to you, so use them wisely mon doux."*

Looking from Benevolence to me to Ezekiel's crumpled lifeless body, JW asked innocently, yet somewhat authoritatively, "Well, Miss Pumpkin, can you let us know what you think happened to Mr. Beals, then?" I didn't interrupt JW as I had to let him have some investigative duty in the matter before us.

Benevolence placed another heaping spoon of pickled beets on my plate and then responded to JW. "Well, I don't know, Deputy Riley," Benevolence chuckled a bit out loud and continued. "Ever think maybe he just gave up? Tired of fighting against me all these years, just gave in, knowing my mama's love for me was always greater than hers for him. Maybe he just up and killed himself knowing he didn't have the power over me anymore. I didn't hear anything from outside when I went back into the garden, except . . ." Benevolence hesitated a moment, "well, just that ole kitchen screen door slamming behind itself . . ."

JW slowly placed his fork down on my plate with a portion of pickled beets still on its prongs, and cocked his head a bit quizzically and clearly disbelieving, while he looked at me and then at Benevolence directly and said, "Wait a minute, Miss Pumpkin, you mean when you left to go outside to the garden after you put the butcher knife back in the knife draw," he said, tapping his right forefinger on the oval, oak kitchen table, "that's when you remember hearing the kitchen screen door close behind itself?"

Benevolence gave me a deep, penetrating, *knowing* gaze and then spoke with a measured tone to JW. "No, sir. When I was already out in Mama's vegetable-rose garden, I was bending over, picking up my pole beans with my backside to the house and that's when I heard the kitchen screen door slam shut again."

JW looked at me in disbelief. "I know what it sounds like, JW," I said to him trying to figure out myself how I was going to explain these seemingly absurd things to him.

Then with uncontained excitement, JW declared, "Good God, Sheriff Roulette, listening to Miss Pumpkin's story I almost forgot," and reaching into his pocket, JW handed me

51

a small piece of note paper. "I think you may want to see this."

As JW handed me the note paper he retorted, "I found it in there . . ." motioning with a tilt of his head to the living room. "And the other thing, you know it's odd," his voice trailed off a bit, "all the while I was in the living room, it smelled real sweet in there. At first, I thought like gardenias but that was too sweet for those . . . what you call those bushes with little tube-like white and yellow flowers down here? You know Miss Benevolence was talking about smelling them earlier."

"Honeysuckle," Benevolence and I said simultaneously.

"Yeah, honeysuckle. My Auntie Tilly has them too. That's what it smells like in there . . . " JW again tilted his head in the direction of the living room.

Benevolence and I looked at each other in silence as small details moved together in our minds, slowly fitting together like pieces of a puzzle. I read the piece of paper deliberately and then, looking across at JW, I pensively asked, "Where did you find this, JW?" as I handed the piece of paper to Benevolence.

"It was on the floor tucked underneath Miss Beauty's side table that was knocked over. I could smell that honeysuckle getting heavier and heavier in the living room, like that smell was leading me somewhere. That's strange, right?" JW shook his head slightly in confusion.

"Hmm, I combed every inch of the hardwoods when I was in the living room, and I never saw this, JW . . . that's interesting," I answered pensively.

"Maybe you weren't the one meant to find it, Sheriff Louie," Benevolence said with a smile as she held the small piece of paper, her eager eyes reviewing each line on the page. Then, with joyful amazement, she looked up at the young deputy and announced, "This is my mama's handwriting, Deputy." Benevolence looked over to me while waving the piece of paper in the air like a victory flag, "This is my mama's message to me . . . and maybe to the three of us!"

I answered with careful thought, "That's your mother's handwriting all right, Benevolence; I would know Beauty's handwriting anywhere. But how in the world did I miss this?"

"I told you she was there standing over my shoulder. It *was* Mama! She left this for *all* of us, Sheriff Louie, and you too, Deputy!" Benevolence said excitedly.

"Me? Why would your mother want me to see that or find it?" JW asked Benevolence in complete bewilderment and denial.

"Well, maybe because Mama believes it's time for you to begin knowing something about Heavenly things if you're going to work down here in the Delta, young Deputy," Benevolence said to JW flatly and matter-a-factly.

Then Benevolence began reading out loud what was written on the paper as the three of us sat at her kitchen table.

It's your time, my little baby girl. He was just a big ole sad, lonely, and ungrateful bully to you. I took care of him . . . it's all yours now, without a worry of ole Ezekiel berating you on every turn—all of it yours! Just like I always told you, baby girl!

Benevolence laid down the piece of paper on her kitchen table and patted it gently and proclaimed with great authority, "Yes, Sheriff, that's who done him in and that's what the sound of the screen door slamming the second time was, when I was out in Mama's vegetable-rose garden."

The young deputy, bewildered and awestruck, looked at Benevolence. "Wait a minute, Miss Pumpkin. Are you saying your mother, who's been dead since you were ten years old—what, now, twenty-one years?—killed Mr. Beals and then wrote that note leaving it for you, and then walked out that screen door!?" JW looked away from Benevolence, pointing to the kitchen screen door.

"No," Benevolence murmured under her breath, with a whimsical smile and raised eyebrows, looking straight at JW. "Well, probably more like she floated out the screen door, Deputy."

"Miss Pumpkin, all due respect, ma'am, how do we know that handwriting is your mother's?" JW with impatience continued, "I know I'm new around here and I got a lot to learn about things down here in the Mississippi Delta, but you're telling us that your mother—who's been dead since you were a child—came back to kill Mr. Beals? A full-fledged ghost killed him with the butcher knife that you said you put back in the kitchen draw? Good God, ma'am, I'm not sure I buy all this, Miss Pumpkin!" JW pointed to Ezekiel's stiffening body on the living room floor.

I watched as Benevolence stood up from the kitchen table and folded the note slowly and carefully before slipping it in the pocket of her apron. With plate and silverware in hand, Benevolence walked soberly to the kitchen sink and placed her dishes there. She watched from her kitchen window the branches of the weeping willow swaying slowly back and forth as they caught the breeze coming up from the Gulf. The sweet scent of honeysuckle and rose swirled about the kitchen. It was undeniable.

Benevolence turned to me and said with a firm tone, "Sheriff Louie, I do believe it's time to take that ole tattered and torn Dixie flag down," as she nodded to the flag pole that had stood beside the weeping willow tree for years.

Then, she looked at JW with a piercing gaze and with the same unyielding tone, declared to him, "And Deputy Riley, I guess you will just have to do your duty and investigate it all, but believe me, you're not going to find anything here but what you've found already."

"Miss Pumpkin, I just don't understand. You believe your mother came back from the grave to kill Mr. Beals?"

"Well, son, all I'm gonna say to you is sometimes you don't have to understand — you just have to believe it's so. You'll come to know this with a few more years down here in the Delta."

"I'll see about taking that flag down, Benevolence, before I leave today." I offered while still enjoying Benevolence's meal.

Benevolence noticed dust gathering and swirling from someone driving down the dirt road that led to the three-story house on the marsh in Cyprus Groves.

"Somebody's coming, Sheriff."

"I imagine that well be the medical examiner, Benevolence." I pushed myself away from the table and, rising, said to her, "Mighty fine meal, Benevolence; nobody in Jackson County can match your cornbread, that's for sure." I walked over to the kitchen sink to hand Benevolence my dishes, "Always appreciate your hospitality," then I motioned to JW, "come on, JW, hurry up; let's go meet Doc Beauford."

As JW and I were leaving Benevolence's kitchen, JW said to me with surprise, "Hey, Sheriff, do you smell that? It's that scent again . . . that honeysuckle flower like I smelled when I was investigating in the living room."

Already having noticed it, I looked at JW without a word to him and just motioned to my young deputy to follow me to greet the medical examiner just arriving in the driveway. And, as I turned to leave the kitchen, I stopped short at the screen door as I felt something softly brush my shoulder, and from the corner of my eye, I was sure I saw a tall, slender, smoky configuration. I was engulfed with the sweet, soft, swirling aroma of honeysuckle and roses. I looked over at Benevolence and she said to me smiling . . .

"I know, Sheriff Louie, she's here," Benevolence deeply inhaled the sweet fragrance of honeysuckle and rose as it swooshed around her as well. "And I'm gonna be all right now. Your done with me and your business here is over, and I believe you know that."

At that moment, I couldn't help but notice I felt a quick and sudden rush of heartache for the loss of a kind, gentle, and gracious woman we buried years ago and who had befriended me—a young stranger and newly appointed sheriff of Jackson County, Mississippi, who was still grieving the loss of his beautiful, young wife, trying to escape his own sadness to the deep southern Delta of Mississippi. And yet, as quickly as that heartache came upon me, it vanished, and a rush of contentment came over me and that inexplicable *knowing* that the ever-present sadness of Miss Beauty Pumpkin was finally liberated too and put to rest. My French Cajun grand-mère's tender, teaching voice swirled in my head. *"Sometimes, mon amour, a Spirit guards another left behind and crosses over the Celestial veil to see to it that an injustice has been righted and a broken heart mended."* I *knew* at that moment. *We are not going to find anything leading to Benevolence killing old Ezekiel. No. What couldn't be done during Beauty's earthly lifetime was done by her crossing over the Celestial veil. Her daughter is free now. Benevolence is truly free.* I looked around Benevolence's kitchen one more time for something solid to rest my eyes upon before I capitulated to the majesty of it all . . . even though I *knew* and trusted what had taken place. I thought silently to myself, *Time for you to go on now from this place, Miss Beauty. She's safe now.*

ഇ‌ഇ‌ഇ

I knew that some of those *good, Christian,* White folks would be crumbling and hounding me for a while. *"Sheriff Roulette, how come you let that Black girl go free after killing Ezekiel?"* and the well-meaning Delta Black folks would be fine with Benevolence cause they would believe that she just had 'nough and put the Mississippi-Delta "chicken claw death spell" on Ezekiel. What happened on this hot August Mississippi afternoon would eventually fade in folks' minds, and then I'd be getting calls about somebody stole somebody's alligator meat they had drying in their shed and Reverend Wilson would be calling me soon enough cause the money from the Sunday morning collection plate he gave Deacon Macon to deposit at the bank came up short again; *"Go arrest that sinner of a deacon, Sheriff Louie, cause he probably used the money to buy moonshine again from the Wilbe brothers still they got down river."* Yes, things would get back to normal sheriffing soon enough and nobody would be bothering about Benevolence.

ഇ‌ഇ‌ഇ

Leaning against the kitchen sink, Benevolence instructed me, "Now, before you two head back to town, you go and cut yourself some of those long-stem roses from Mama's vegetable-rose garden to brighten up that dreary sheriff's office of yours. And get that JW to pick you two some pole beans too."

57

I smiled to myself as I heard in Benevolence's tone, the same kindness her mother always had extended to me.

"Come on, JW, let's not keep the doc waiting."

ꍧꍧꍧ

I heard the squeaky kitchen screen door slam shut behind Sheriff Louie, and I watched him from the kitchen sink window walk away with his characteristic slight limp into the sweltering Mississippi heat. I noticed the sound of that slamming screen door didn't take my thoughts anywhere this time but to the thought that I needed to put 10W-40 on those rusty old hinges.

I turned and saw the young deputy as he gulped down the last piece of my honey-baked ham and, getting up from the kitchen table, he grabbed himself another large square of my cornbread. As he was headed to the kitchen screen door, I looked over at him and said, "Deputy, every spring and summer, all around this house, grows honeysuckle vines with their fragrant, delicate, little flowers, and out back in my mama's vegetable-rose garden, those dazzling red floribunda roses are in full bloom. See, when my mama was alive, she'd make a beautiful twined garland of both and neatly set it atop her hair. And wherever my mama went, everyone near her would get caught up in the sweet smell of those honeysuckle flowers and the red floribunda roses in her hair. When you smelled the sweet soft fragrance of honeysuckle and drop-dead roses, why, you knew it was my mama coming . . ."

I turned my back to JW, took the folded paper out of my apron pocket, placed it gingerly on the windowsill over the kitchen sink, and said, "Now, Mama, every morning, you are right here with me at my kitchen sink. And just like you told me *this* house and *all* the land around me is mine, now that he's gone."

In an instant, I noticed the sweet scent of honeysuckle and roses that had flooded the living room and kitchen that lazy Mississippi August afternoon had vanished as quickly as it had arrived.

I heard the kitchen screen door gently close behind Deputy J. W. Riley, and through my open kitchen window, I watched him walk briskly toward Sheriff Louie, who was greeting the medical examiner. But then I noticed he stopped suddenly in his stride, turned abruptly toward the open kitchen window, and fixed his eyes on me; it was clear something had instantly struck his comprehension. Like a strike of lightning when a brilliant flash of heat waves fill a room and makes you jump, the puzzle became whole to him. I saw on JW's face a simultaneous expression of disbelief and a striking awakening awareness of the *possibility* of my own mother's visitation—a heavenly angel or specter presence. I *knew* at that moment that young Deputy J. W. Riley had connected it all. With a profound furrowed brow and look of amazement, his mouth broke into an apprehensive smile my way, slowly and respectfully tipped his hat to me, and then turned and walked away. I thought to myself, *Hmph . . . maybe that Yankee boy's gonna be all right with a bit more time down here in the Delta. Yes, that JW just might be okay. What do you think, Mama?*

I turned on the water to wash our supper dishes, and I felt the warm sudsy water on my fingertips from the kitchen tap. It was then I was taken to a sweet memory of when my mama took me on a holiday trip to the ocean for the first time in my life. I was just five years old when we traveled by car on US 45 to Highway 10 then to 98, all the way down the Gulf of Mexico to Apalachicola, Florida, to visit my Aunt Bitty Pumpkin. My mama had drawn our route on a map with a red pencil and told me, "Now, Benevolence, you're going to be my copilot, and you trace your finger on those state routes right there," Mama would point to the red lines. "You make sure you help us stay on course . . . that's your job, little girl. Highway 45 to Highway 10 and then to 98. That is going be carrying us straight to your Auntie Bitty's doorstep."

To make good time, Mama didn't stop at any roadside diner for dinner or supper. Mama knew we wouldn't be served anyway because we were Black, even though Mama had her Green Book for the trip—she wanted to just keep on driving. Even then, I *knew* for her it was like she was a horse that had been bound up in a stable for days and was suddenly set free and wanted to just keep running for miles. But most of all, Mama knew it was also a matter of our safety. For in the deep South, in the early 1960s, even a Black woman driving alone in the daytime with her child by her side through the *Sundown Towns* of Mississippi, Alabama, and Florida . . . well, we were at risk for being pulled over by any White person, and in a flash could disappear, never to be heard from again. So Mama kept driving all through the night. I could tell she was relieved when night fell, cause she leaned back and relaxed in the driver's seat, loosening the tight grip she'd kept on the sterring wheel all day.

So, on our adventure to Apalachicola, Florida, Mama and I happily ate sandwiches along the way that she had neatly and tightly packed in folded cellophane. Mama would say to me, *"I'm going drive us nice and slow so we can enjoy this here ride and let the good Lord carry us safely to your Auntie Bitty's."* We would sing songs and laugh together and Mama told me all kinds of stories like the one about how the little bunny had outsmarted that big ole mean, cantankerous bear. That was my favorite one.

Yes, a six-and-a-half-hour car drive of sheer bliss, just me and Mama, free . . . the both of us free from Cypress Groves and all that went with it. I remembered feeling wrapped in the softness of my mother's presence like no other time. On that road trip to Apalachicola, I watched new places roll by as I looked out the car window; so different than the marshlands of Cypress Grove and the cotton fields that surrounded us. I was excited to learn there were places other than dusty ole Cypress Groves, Mississippi. How I loved being in the ocean for my very first time! Splashing in the rushing waves of the Gulf waters - those tepid, warm, turquoise ocean waters going on and on for miles as far as I could see . On the ocean's edge, it was all so exhilarating and peaceful so different than the Mississippi Delta where Mama and I lived.

And then when we had finally arrived at Auntie Bitty's . . . well the ruckus began. My mama and Auntie Betti's endless hearty laughter was contagious. I would start laughing too, although I didn't know what was so funny about the stories they were telling each other. I never remembered my mama laughing so much as when was with Auntie Bitty - her oldest sister. When the two of them were together, why, they laughed and laughed so hard that tears of joy kept rolling down their cheeks and they'd be holding their sides and slapping their hands on their knees with uncontrollable laughter. I would look at them both in their moments of glee, and I knew they both were intertwined in sisterly devotion for one another as tight as the weave on a Gullah Sweetgrass basket—so powerful, there was not a person or circumstance that could break it—and surely not even *him*! My mama was happy then; a blissful free happiness I'd never seen or felt her experience before, and especially not when we were with Mr. Ezekiel Beals.

To this day, I still liked the way the sound of how the name of that town rolled on my tongue and lips. I said it aloud slowly to myself at the kitchen sink and listened to its name ring in my ears. *Ap . . . a . . . lach . . . i . . . cola. Hmm . . . sure is pretty.* I sighed to myself. Everything was happier when my mama was still alive. I turned from the kitchen sink, dried my hands with the kitchen towel that was tucked into the belt on my flowered shirt dress, and walked out into the heat of a Mississippi summer day to my mama's vegetable-rose garden and thought, *Mama, maybe I'll drive myself down to Ap . . . a . . . lach . . . i . . . cola. Yes, that's sho 'nuff what I'm going to do! Going to take US 45 to Highway 10 to Highway 98 . . . and then right to Auntie Bitty's doorstep. Would be nice to be with real family again . . . and laugh together till we cry tears of joy that roll down our cheeks, just like you two used to do, Mama.*

ຂຄຂຄຂຄ

Acknowledgments

I would like to thank the remarkable creative team at BookLogix, who helped to see this book to its final completion. From cover design to scrutinizing every period and comma, without each of your steadfast, dynamic inputs and genuine interest, my rough-draft pages would not have been realized into becoming the compelling and entertaining story I always wanted to tell in *Honeysuckle and Roses*.

About the Author

Jody Anne Iodice grew up on a rural country farm wandering the pastures for hours—dotted with its cows and baby calves, horses and their fillies and colts, dogs and their puppies, and her pet pig—all the while creating imaginative stories in her mind with a host of colorful characters. Since childhood, the author has always been a keen observer of the most intricate aspects of people and their surroundings; this set the stage for her fiction writing.

When "Dr. Jody," is not working in her clinical private practice of thirty-two years, teaching master and PhD candidates in clinical and forensic science courses, or developing and facilitating integrative complementary oncology medicine programs at Piedmont hospital in Atlanta, Georgia, she spends her spare time doing one of the most enjoyable things she has done since childhood: engrossing herself in contemplation weaving tales full of robust characters, different eras in time, and beguiling locations setting the stage for her next novella or short story.

www.ingramcontent.com/pod-product-compliance
Lightning Source LLC
Chambersburg PA
CBHW050428110726
47899CB00008B/2890